Herbert Pelham Curtis

Uncle Robert

Or, Love's Labor Saved. A comedy in three Acts

Herbert Pelham Curtis

Uncle Robert
Or, Love's Labor Saved. A comedy in three Acts

ISBN/EAN: 9783743419902

Manufactured in Europe, USA, Canada, Australia, Japa

Cover: Foto ©Andreas Hilbeck / pixelio.de

Manufactured and distributed by brebook publishing software
(www.brebook.com)

CAST OF CHARACTERS.

Boston Museum, 1861.

UNCLE ROBERT SINGLE,...........aged 65,........Mr. Warren.

JOHN GRAMPUS,.................... "   50,........ "   McClannin.

EDWARD, ⎫   ⎧ "   25,........ "   Wilson.

PATTY, ⎬ *his Children,*...... ⎨ "   17,........Miss Reignolds.

WILLIAM, ⎭   ⎩ "   16, ...Miss Josephine Orton.

BROWNJOHN, *Patty's Lover,* .... "   27,........Mr. Mestayer.

DION, *Servant,*......................................——

LOUISA CARLYLE, *Housekeeper,* ... "   20,........Miss Annie Clark.

COSTUMES.

UNCLE ROBERT. Loose coat; breeches; gaiters; white cravat.
GRAMPUS. Gray trowsers; dark body-coat; dark cravat.
EDWARD. Riding suit; whip, &c.
WILLIAM. Jacket and trowsers; turned-over collar.
BROWNJOHN. Gentleman's dress; gray trowsers; gloves.
DION. Livery — plain.

PATTY. Young girl's dress, rather short skirts.
LOUISA. White or light-colored dress — simple.

OR,

LOVE'S LABOR SAVED.

A Comedy.—In Three Acts.

BY

H. P. CURTIS.

With Original Cast, Costumes, and all the Stage Business.

BOSTON:
WILLIAM V. SPENCER,
94 WASHINGTON STREET.

Herbert Pelham Curtis

Uncle Robert

UNCLE ROBERT:

OR,

LOVE'S LABOR SAVED.

ACT I.

SCENE I. — *Parlor in* GRAMPUS' *house, handsomely furnished.* — *Doors* R., L., *and* C.

LOUISA *and* WILLIAM *discovered.* — LOUISA *sits at side, winding worsted from* WILLIAM'S *hands.* — *On table near her a tambour frame.*

Louisa. We had better stop now, Mr. William. You will be tired.

William. Tired! How could I be tired doing *anything* for you? I would pass through fire for *your* sake, Louisa! (*Very tenderly.*)

Lou. (*laughing*). Would you, really?

Wil. Can you doubt it? I wish a fire might break out in the house this very night —

Lou. For shame, sir! —

Wil. The flames rush to heaven! — Beams are crashing! — rafters tumbling! Suddenly you throw open an upper window, and shriek for assistance! The stairs are on fire! — nobody dares enter the house! You are lost! —

Lou. Hush, for Heaven's sake! You terrify me!

Wil. But no, not quite lost. I, I am at hand! I rush in — break open your door — carry you out in my arms! — You are saved! (*Seizes her in his arms.*)

Lou. (*pushing him away.*) Be quiet, please. None of that; — you 'll tangle my worsted.

Wil. Or I wish you would fall into the pond. How delightful to jump in after you — save you — dive for you — recover your body —

Lou. Recover your own senses, this instant, or we shall never wind this worsted. (*Laughing*) You have an extraordinary desire, it seems, to have me perish by fire or water.

Wil. Perish! Oh, Louisa! for a chance to save your life! Oh, for an opportunity to do you some prodigious service! — deliver you from robbers — save you from run-away horses — protect you from mad dogs! I can think, dream, of nothing but how I can best prove to you the extent of the adoration, — the burning adoration —

Lou. (*taking the skein*). Stop, stop, Mr. William; — enough of this nonsense. You are too old to behave so like a child.

Wil. A child! I am *not* a child.

Lou. (*laughing*). And only fourteen.

Wil. (*proudly*). I'm almost sixteen.

Lou. So much the worse, then. I must give up petting you immediately.

Wil. Ah, dearest Louisa! call me child, then, forever.

Lou. I'm afraid you read too many silly novels, Mr. William. (*They advance.*)

Wil. Novels? Oh no — yes — no — that is — I must make myself familiar with American literature, of course, you know; — Ned Buntline, and G. P. R. James, and Sylvanus Cobb, and Mrs. Stowe, and the Lamplighter, and the Ledger, and — Ah, Louisa, if you know the adoration that fills — (*Kneels.*)

Lou. Stand up at once, sir. Mr. William, I must request you, seriously, to use a different tone towards me. You must always address me as Miss Carlyle. (*She* x's *L.*) I always call you Mr. William, and —

Wil. (*alarmed*). Are you angry with me?

Lou. What would your father say, if he heard you talking such nonsense to me as you do?

Wil. Ah, Louis — Miss Carlyle, I mean — don't mention father; — anything else you please; — the horrors of conscience, — anything; but don't, *don't* speak of *him*.

Lou. Your uncle, then?

Wil. Uncle Robert? Oh, that's a very different thing, — another affair altogether. Speak of him as much as you like.

Lou. Tell me, Mr. William, what relation is old Mr. Single to the family? I've been here a month, now, but I don't know the actual relationship yet.

Wil. Oh, well; let's think; I don't know exactly, myself. On my mother's side, somehow, I believe. Very distant, at any rate.

Lou. He seems to be a very good old gentleman; — so kind and obliging.

Wil. He's the best old chap that ever lived. Ever since mother died he's had the whole management of us children. He's a real old brick, I assure you. Everybody depends on him in this house. If any of us gets into a scrape we always run right to him. And he has to interpose between us children and father pretty often, too; for father is *so* savage sometimes. (*Tenderly*) But *you* need no protector.

Lou. Fie, Mr. William; no nonsense.

Wil. Even father's severity is soothed by the loveliness of your disposition.

Lou. Mr. William, I requested you, only a minute ago — (x *to* R.)

Wil. Oh, Louisa! if you could only conceive my devotion to you! Do you remember what the poet says? —

> " His beaming eyes o'erflow with love,
> Freely the tear of rapture runs,
> And wandering pensive in the grove,
> His brothers' noisy sports he shuns.

"Her steps the mantling blush awake;
　Her greeting fills his heart with light;
　The fairest *flowers* he culls to deck
　　The pathway where —"

Lou. (*turning suddenly*). Oh, Mr. William! this is dreadful! — this is dreadful! Oh, I hope I'm mistaken —

Wil. About what?

Lou. Your father and your uncle have been complaining, for a week past, of thefts in the flower-garden; and every morning I find a fresh bouquet in my chamber, and never can discover who places it there. Oh, Mr. William —

Wil. But, Louisa — Miss Carlyle —

Lou. It is you.

Wil. Dear Miss Carlyle, I assure you —

Lou. You not only expose yourself very foolishly to your father's just anger —

Wil. Oh, please don't! —

Lou. But you expose me, too, to serious misconstruction. What *would* they think?

Wil. (*humbly*). I never thought of that.

Lou. I gave you credit, young as you are, for more reflection, — more common sense.

Wil. Oh, Louisa! pray, pray forgive me.

Lou. Not unless you solemnly promise, in future —

Enter GRAMPUS, EDWARD, *and* PATTY, C.

Grampus (*very kindly, advancing*). He shall promise everything you require, Miss Carlyle.

Lou. (*starting*). Ah! Mr. Grampus.

Gr. I hope you've been reading him a good lecture.

Lou. Oh, no sir. I — (WILLIAM *looks at her imploringly.*)

Gr. He's been in mischief again, I'm sure.

Lou. No, no, indeed, sir; — indeed he has not.

Gr. (*to* WILLIAM). Go to your room, and study your lessons, at once, sir. And for the future do everything Miss Carlyle tells you. Do you hear?

Wil. Yes, sir.　　　　　　　　　　　　　　　[*Exit*, D. R. H.

Gr. (*All coming forward.*) Martha, have you made those arrangements about the house, with Miss Carlyle, which I spoke of? Do so, instantly.

Patty. I came now to do so, father. Come, if you please, Miss Carlyle; we'll see about them at once.

　　　　　　　　　　　　[*Exeunt* PATTY *and* LOUISA, R. 2 E.

Gr. Edward, go to my library. I have a few instructions to give you. I'll come immediately. I want a few words with uncle, first. (*Takes up a newspaper.*)

Enter UNCLE ROBERT, L. 2 E.

Edward (*aside to* UNCLE ROBERT). Don't go out without seeing me, uncle. I want to speak to you.　　　　[*Exit* L. D. 2 E.

Uncle Robert. Did you want me, Grampus?
1*

Gr. Yes, Single, I want to let you know an arrangement I've made, and also to make you my confidant in a business secret.

U. R. (L.) Business secret? Well, go on ; I'm listening.

Gr. (R.) I'm so convinced that my factory at Cottonville needs more undivided attention than I can give it from this distance, that I've determined to send Edward to live there.

U. R. Edward? You don't say so ! But —

Gr. Well?

U. R. Poor Ned got home only a month ago. He's scarcely had time to turn round yet. It seems to me rather tough to pack him off to Cottonville so soon. Let him enjoy himself a little, before he goes to work again.

Gr. Pooh, pooh ! Young men should work. It'll be time enough for him to enjoy himself when he gets to be *my* age.

U. R. He won't like it much, I fancy.

Gr. Like it or not, he goes. I never stand any nonsense. He sets off in an hour. Enjoyment, indeed ! Pooh, pooh ! Let his rooms remain vacant, for the present, however, till I decide what to do with them.

U. R. Very well.

Gr. In the second place, this constant robbery of my garden vexes me very much. You say you have no trace of the thief?

U. R. Not the faintest.

Gr. Very odd. Your room is in the cottage. The thefts happen under your very nose. Who the deuce can it be? One would think you might not only detect the scoundrel, but catch him too.

U. R. Ha, ha ! I should make a poor thief-taker, I fear, with my gout and my weak eye-sight.

Gr. Well, well ; from to-day let the garden-gate be locked every evening at eight o'clock. Tell the gardener so.

U. R. Certainly, certainly. Is that all?

Gr. No ; now for the most important of all. There's a great quantity of Calcutta goods in store here, now, which can be bought at a very low figure ; for the holders are losing interest on them the whole time. Now, if France and England recognize this infernal bogus Southern Confederacy of ours, these goods are bound to go up ; for that's about the same thing as a declaration of war, they say. Luckily for me, however, nobody believes they will do so. There's no telling about it, you see ; for England can't be trusted in the least. Her proclamation of neutrality shows that plainly enough. The next steamer's news will settle the thing beyond a doubt. It's a capital chance for a speculation, you see. Now, I've sent Tompkins to New York [Boston — Halifax], to get me the latest news from Europe. He's to telegraph me, the instant the steamer arrives, and I've arranged to have all the usual telegraphs to the papers delayed an hour. It cost me a mint of money, but if things turn out as I expect, it'll pay, and pay well. If I should happen to be out when the telegram comes, the messenger is to give it to *you*. It'll have no address on it, for safety's sake. As soon as it comes, send and hunt me up, *wherever* I am. The greatest secrecy is absolutely essential, you perceive ; — no one but you knows an iota of the business. So be sure you mind what you do.

U. R. Ay, ay, Grampus, I understand. Trust me for that.

Gr. (x *to* L). Very well. That's all, I think. I'll go, now, and pack off Edward. [*Exit* L. D. 2 E.

U. R. Always scheming and speculating. He's got a handsome fortune already, and wants to double it. Well, well ; if everybody were as I am, I suppose the world would soon come to a stand-still. Poor Ned! how bored he'll be in that horrid Cottonville! Well, well, well ; I must be off ; no time to waste.

Wil. (*pulling his head in at* R. 2. E.) Pst — Uncle Robert, are you alone?

U. R. Yes, scamp, I am. What now?

Wil. (*coming in*). Oh, uncle! — dear, darling uncle —

U. R. What's the matter now?

Wil. (*coaxingly*). Uncle Robert, you must help me instantly.

U. R. Speak out, lad ; what's the trouble?

Wil. (*softly*). I've got to stay after school, three days running.

U. R. Scapegrace! what have you been up to now?

Wil. Oh, uncle, hardly anything. I want you to fix it so father shan't suspect me. You know he always makes such an awful row.

U. R. Well, but won't he miss you from the table?

Wil. If he notices it, tell him I've been invited out ; or say you sent me on an errand. Make some nice, good excuse for me.

U. R. William, when do you mean to begin to be a steady boy?

Wil. Oh, Uncle Bob! preach some other time, please. Promise me you'll help me through this scrape ; now do!

U. R. Not unless you tell me what you've been doing, sir.

Wil. Oh, a mere nothing, uncle. I was reading the Arabian Days' Entertainments, under my desk, and the teacher caught me at it ; that's all.

U. R. Now, see the consequences of this vile novel-reading. And I've forbidden it so often, too.

Wil. Don't find fault with me *all* the time, Uncle Bob. I know old folks say a boy should be always cultivating his mind ; (*affectedly*) but the heart, the *heart* has its rights.

U. R. The heart! Ha, ha, ha! What do *you* know about the heart?

Wil. (*offended*). Why do you talk to me as if I were a little baby, Uncle Robert? Feel here, — see how rough my beard is.

U. R. Ha, ha, ha! — rough as sandpaper. So it is. The heart, forsooth! The lad talks of his heart! Ha, ha, ha!

Wil. Of course I do. I have a precious secret there, *I* can tell you.

U. R. Ha, ha, ha! a precious secret! You vagabond!

Wil. Don't you believe it? Oh, uncle, if you only knew — (*Pauses.*)

U. R. Knew what? Come, come, Willie, don't be a fool.

Wil. A fool! Uncle Robert, you're real mean.

U. R. Fol de rol! 'Pon my word! So your head's turned with novel-reading already, is it?

Wil. (*sentimentally*). Ah! does it need novels to excite emotions of love in the susceptible heart?

U. R. Ha, ha, ha! This is *too* much. Tell me, lad, have you se-
lected your sweetheart yet?

Wil. If you'll promise not to tell —

U. R. I'm all curiosity!

Wil. Promise me you'll never tell.

U. R. Well, I promise. Now for it ; — who is she?

Wil. (*whispering*). Miss Carlyle.

U. R. What! Why, you little demon!

Wil. Oh, Uncle Robert, who can control the aspirations of his
heart? She is *so* beautiful! Her bright blue eyes beam with such
rays of heaven! Her liquid voice is such enchanting music!

U. R. Stop, stop! Ha, ha, ha! And what does Miss Carlyle say
to this? Does she accept your addresses?

Wil. Uncle Robert, do you think I could have the courage to
breathe a syllable of it to her? No, no ; it's enough for me to wor-
ship her in silence. Oh, uncle! I love her *so* deeply! I could die
for her! — I could strew her path with roses, lilies, violets! — I
could — (*Walks theatrically to* L.)

U. R. (*seizing his ear*). Rascal! I've got you!

Wil. Ow! ow! ow! Uncle Robert, let go!

U. R. You're the *thief!* — *you* stole our flowers, sir.

Wil. Hush! don't speak so loud. No, no, I didn't. It wasn't
I, at all.

U. R. (*dropping his voice*). It *is* you, sir. It can be nobody else.

Wil. I assure you, Uncle Robert —

U. R. Fiddle de dee! don't fib. You can't get off. Now, I'll
not tell of you this time ; but if ever you do so again, — if I find a
single bud gone, — I'll expose you to your father. Now mind.

Wil. Oh, Uncle Bob! you couldn't be so mean.

U. R. Besides, you scamp, it would be better if you'd attend
more to your Cicero, and leave story-books to your elders. Bring
me that book you spoke of, sir, at once. I've heard of it before.

Wil. (*coaxing*). Uncle Robert, you'll help me along with father
now, won't you? Alas! I shan't see her at dinner for three whole
days. But her image is printed on my heart! I will think of her,
and be happy! (*Coaxing*) Uncle Robert, that about the flowers,
now, is a secret, you know. Father has so much to do, it would be
too bad to trouble him with that. Now, remember, I've told you
my secret. Your heart is too noble, too generous, to betray it. Be
sure not to tell ; — you've promised. Good bye.

[*Exit, running,* C. D.

U. R. Hallo, good-for-naught! where now? Clever lad, Willie.
So full of life and spirit. And so he's in love. Ha, ha, ha!
·(*Sadly*) Ah, it's a delightful feeling! Heigh-ho! William will be
more plucky than I was, I fancy. I never could quite make up my
mind ; so now I'm nothing but a tedious, tiresome old bachelor.
Rather early for the boy. Trouble may come of it. No, no ; no
danger. An early love affair is an excellent thing for a boy like him,
— keeps him steady, and all that. However, I'll keep my eye on
him.

Pat. (*putting her head in at* R. H. 2 E.) Hsh! — uncle!

U. R. (*looking round*). Eh?

Pat. Hush ! Has father gone out?

U. R. What now? Yes.

Pat. (*running down*). Oh, I 'm so thankful !

U. R. What 's the matter?

Pat. I want to make you my confidant.

U. R. Confidant?

Pat. Yes. (*Nods vehemently.*)

U. R. Indeed ! Very well.

Pat. I 'm — afraid — you 'll laugh, uncle.

U. R. What?

Pat. Must I speak?

U. R. Why, my dear, if you want to make me your confidant, I 'm afraid you must.

Pat. Is it possible you can't guess?

U. R. Guess? Not I. How should I guess?

Pat. Heigh-ho !

U. R. Indeed, my dear, I 'm not given to guessing ; and if you won't speak —

Pat. Well, if I must, then — Turn away your head. (*Whispers*) I 'm in love.

U. R. Ha, ha, ha! In love!

Pat. (*stopping his mouth*). Don't speak so loud.

U. R. You — in love !

Pat. (*pettishly*). Yes, Uncle Robert, I 'm in love.

U. R. Ha, ha, ha! Let 's take a look at you, and see how you look when you 're in love.

Pat. Pooh, uncle! how unkind you are !

U. R. Nay, darling, all the good we old folks can get out of you young lovers is the fun of a little banter. Well, who 's the happy man?

Pat. Now, Uncle Robert —

U. R. Well.

Pat. Have you, really and truly, observed nothing?

U. R. Nothing whatever.

Pat. (*whispering*). Julius.

U. R. Julius?

Pat. Mr. Brownjohn !

U. R. Oh ! ah ! — he 's Julius, is he? I was n't aware. Hem ! — ha ! — yes. Well ; handsome fellow, Brownjohn. I 've often noticed him.

Pat. Oh, thank you, uncle, thank you. He *is* handsome, is n't he?

U. R. But stop, Patty ; seems to me that since Miss Carlyle has been with us, he 's been showing *her* a great *deal* of attention. How 's that?

Pat. That 's a part of our plan.

U. R. Eh?

Pat. Yes ; you see, uncle, we 've been acquainted with each other ever so long, — six weeks, — and engaged three. He 's a young merchant, and not very well off yet, though he has enough to satisfy *me*, I 'm sure. So we 've never ventured to tell father yet ; for he 's so prejudiced, you know. He says I shall never marry any one whose fortune is n't as large as the one he means to give me. So, what can we do?

U. R. It's a difficult question for a pair of young lovers, 'faith.

Pat. Now, dear, darling uncle, do give us your advice.

U. R. Well, but I don't know what advice to give you. What can I do for you? Now, if I had any money —

Pat. No, no, not that. We want you to prepare father to learn our engagement, — let fall a word or two, now and then, about what a fine fellow Julius is, you know. He *is* a fine fellow, uncle, really.

U. R. Indeed! Is it possible?

Pat. Yes, really and truly ; — that is — on one single point — I 'm not quite —

U. R. Eh?

Pat. I 'll tell you the whole story, uncle. You see, it might excite father's suspicions to see Julius coming here every day or two, you know ; so we agreed he should pretend to be devoting himself to Miss Carlyle.

U. R. Oho! that 's the reason, is it? But that was very naughty in you, Patty.

Pat. But it seems to me, sometimes, as if — as if —

U. R. (*laughing*). As if he played his part too well, eh?

Pat. And have *you* observed it too? Then my suspicions were correct.

U. R. Ha, ha, ha! Patty, jealous already!

Pat. Oh, no, Uncle Robert, not *jealous* in the least. But still, Louisa is such a flirt —

U. R. (*shaking his head*). Louisa a flirt! Oh, fye, Patty! take care — take care.

Pat. Yes, uncle, a dreadful flirt. Oh dear! I see you 've taken her into favor, like all the rest.

U. R. Ha, ha, ha! true, Patty, true ; she 's bewitched us all, I believe.

Pat. And can you laugh and joke, uncle, when I 'm in such a state of anxiety to obtain your advice and assistance?

U. R. Nay, darling ; what would you have me do?

Pat. Oh, uncle, you must help us all you possibly can. Watch Miss Carlyle, and tell me if you make any discoveries. And if Julius and I should happen to want a *tête à tête* —

U. R. You expect me to give you the opportunity? Child, child, it goes against my conscience.

Pat. No, no, no, it does n't, if you really mean to help us. I shall never be happy in this world without my Julius. Dear fellow! Father will oppose our marriage only through his prejudices ; and you know, Uncle Robert, how very unreasonable prejudiced people are.

U. R. (*aside*). How cunningly the little serpent argues! Minx!

Pat. (*coaxingly*). I knew I should n't be deceived, in making you my confidant, uncle. You 'll help us, now, won't you?

U. R. Hush ; I hear your father coming.

Pat. Quick, uncle, your hand on it.

U. R. You torment! how dare you? Don't hurry me.

Pat. Your hand, your hand! Promise to keep our secret, and help us.

U. R. Well — there.

Pat. Oh, thanks, Uncle Robert, thanks! Dear, darling uncle! Now everything will go right. [*Exit* R. 2 E.

U. R. Humph! — Brownjohn! Well, I never heard anything against him. The little snake is right, — her father is brimful of prejudices. Well, well, well, I'll see what I can do for her.

Enter GRAMPUS, L. D., *hat and cane in hand.*

Gr. (*speaking off*). Good-bye, Edward. You understand my arrangements. Pleasant journey to you! (*Comes forward.*) Edward is getting ready the necessary articles, and starts immediately.

U. R. Very good. (*Aside*) Poor fellow!

Gr. The directions I gave you, a few minutes since —

U. R. Shall be attended to; depend on me. (GRAMPUS *goes up* C., *and comes down* R.)

Gr. By the way, uncle, I feel like making you my confidant.

U. R. Confidant! Ha, ha, ha! This makes number three! Ha, ha!

Gr. Three what?

U. R. Hem! hem! — I mean you 've made me your confidant twice already. Hem!

Gr. Ah! have I? Ha, ha! true. Come, uncle, in confidence, now, what 's your opinion — hem! — your opinion of — our new housekeeper?

U. R. Miss Carlyle?

Gr. Yes. (*Simpers.*)

U. R. Well, she does well enough; — I think means well. And she 's quite pretty, too; eh?

Gr. Pretty! Is that all? She 's lovely, Single, — perfectly lovely?

U. R. Hallo! I say, Grampus —

Gr. Observe her delicate foot, her taper waist, her soft hand! and what a neck and shoulders she has! and what a swan-like walk! Eh?

U. R. Why, Grampus! Grampus!

Gr. I see what you 're thinking about. Well, you can't say I 'm not in the prime of life, Single. I — I — in fact, uncle, I begin to think I 'm much taken by her.

U. R. (*bursting out laughing*). Ha, ha, ha! Father and son! (*Claps his hand to his mouth.*)

Gr. (*seizing his arm*). Have you noticed it too?

U. R. Noticed what too? I 've noticed nothing.

Gr. Why, that Edward is always casting sheep's eyes at her?

U. R. Edward! (*Aside*) Phew!

Gr. Ay, Edward. My eyes are sharp yet, I tell you. He 's falling in love with her, heels over head; so it 's high time I packed him off to Cottonville.

U. R. So! — so that was the reason?

Gr. Well — hem! — not the only reason —

U. R. To get a rival out of the way! Ha, ha!

Gr. A rival ! Pooh, pooh ! However —

U. R. You were saying — *however* —

Gr. Yes — hem ! hem ! — I 've made no fixed plan as yet ; but — Come, Single, say, yourself ; — here am I, strong, hale, and hearty, and fifty years old. I 've worked like a horse, all my life. Who has any right to object, if I begin to think, now, of enjoying myself a little?

U. R. No one, no one, surely.

Gr. Well, to do that, one must have a companion, you know.

U. R. No doubt, no doubt. Heigh-ho !

Gr. I 'm rich ; and I don't care a fig for what the world will say, you know.

U. R. To be sure. So then, you mean to marry Miss Carlyle, and —

Gr. Pooh, pooh ! not so fast. There 's no *so then* about it. It 's a possibility only, so far.

U. R. Ha, ha, ha ! Grampus, you 've said quite enough.

Gr. (*slapping him on the back*). Ha, ha ! I 've said nothing yet, uncle. But I want you to find out what she thinks of me, if you can. Sound her sentiments a little ; — you understand ; — discover if her affections are engaged to any one else.

U. R. I 'll do it, Grampus, — I 'll do it. It 's the easiest thing in the world, I 've no doubt. These young girls never know how to keep a secret like us old folks. They 've no experience, — no caution. I 'll pump her.

Gr. Good ! good ! Now, one word more. This Brownjohn, who 's been coming and going, here, for the last six weeks. I know nothing against the fellow, and I believe he stands fair as a merchant. But hang him, he shows a great deal too much attention in this quarter.

U. R. Eh? not to Louisa?

Gr. Of course. Why do you start?

U. R. Oh, I — I thought —

Gr. Not my daughter ! By George ! if I thought that, I 'd soon put a spoke in his wheel. (*Walks about.*)

U. R. No, no, no, no. I 've noticed as much myself, lately. He *is* very devoted to Miss Carlyle, no doubt.

Gr. Well, so you think so, too? What shall we do about it ? If you could give a little caution to Miss Carlyle, — let fall a word in my favor, now and then ; praise my kindness of heart, — my sweetness of disposition —

U. R. Ha, ha, ha ! Ay, ay ; trust me for that.

Gr. Now, Single, I depend on you. Keep an eye on Brownjohn, too ; and above all, be as secret as the grave.

U. R. I will, I will ; depend on it.

Gr. Good ! (*Shakes his hand.*) Uncle, if all goes well, you shall never regret it, I promise you.   [*Exit* c. d.

U. R. Queer family, this, 'pon my word ! Ha, ha, ha ! The son in love, the daughter in love, and the father in love. What a wry face William will make, when his sweetheart becomes his mother-in-law ! It 'll read like Don Carlos. However, he 's a mere lad. He 'll soon get over it. If Edward had been the one, now — So he sends the poor fellow off to Cottonville, out of pure jealousy. Too bad !

too bad! Ay, he's a tyrant to his children, so he is. His sweetness
of disposition, forsooth! Ha, ha! Hem!—he's about right,
though;—I begin to like Miss Carlyle as well as the rest of 'em;
and if I thought she could take a fancy to me—

Enter EDWARD *and* LOUISA, L. D. — EDWARD *comes forward*, L.

Ah! what now? Well, Ned, ready to start?
Ed. Uncle, before I go, I want to make you my confidant.
U. R. What! you too? Is all the world going to make me its
confidant? Are you in love, too, you dog?
Ed. Worse yet, uncle. Hush! I'm married.
U. R. Married!—you married! This is a finisher! You mar-
ried!
Ed. Hush!—not so loud! Yes, for the last three months.
U. R. Three months! (*Whispers*) And to whom, you unlucky
fellow,—to whom?
Ed. (*leading forward* LOUISA). To this young lady.
U. R. (*falling into a chair*). Miss Carlyle! Married!
Ed. Louisa, this good gentleman will take care of you while I am
away. Trust to him without fear.
Lou. (*tenderly*, x *to* C.) You despise me, Mr. Single; and with
good reason. (*Weeps.*)
U. R. This is a terrible business! Your father, poor boy—
Ed. He'll be reconciled, by and by, I'm certain.
U. R. And William— (x *to* C.)
Ed. What?
U. R. And Brownjohn—
Ed. What has he to do with it?
U. R. And Patty— Oh, I shall go crazy!
Ed. What do you mean by Patty, and Brownjohn, and—
U. R. Eh? Good gracious! I never mentioned 'em.
Ed. What has Brownjohn to do with my wife?
U. R. Oh, nothing, nothing, of course. Hem! My brain is in
a perfect whirl. Let me get a little composed, for goodness' sake!
Ed. But tell me!
U. R. I can't. I've promised secrecy.
Ed. Secrecy! About what?
U. R. I should let it out, if I told you. What do you want me to
do?
Ed. First promise to be secret.
U. R. Oh dear me! that's just what all the others said.
Ed. Others! What others? And what has Brownjohn to do
with us? You terrify me.
U. R. Nothing, nothing; honor bright. Your wife! Well, well!
How grandly it sounds! Ned, lad, I've long been wishing you'd
bring a nice little wife into the family. It'll cheer us up, when the
little picaninnies— Nay, nay, my dear, don't be vexed. (*Lifts
her head.*) Excellent, Ned, excellent! You've shown your taste.
Lou. I entreat, Mr. Single—
U. R. Nay, darling, oblige me by forgetting my surname. *Uncle*—everybody calls me *uncle*; and you must. But, children, what
2

will be the end of this ?   There 'll be a terrible explosion, when your
father hears of it.

Ed. For the present, then, he must n't hear of it.   All I ask now
is your protection for my wife.   My going to Cottonville has disar-
ranged all my plans.

U. R. Tell me, at once, Ned, how it all came about.

Ed. Very simply.   I came to know Louisa, while managing father's business at Detroit ; and knowing I should never obtain father's
consent, I persuaded her to consent to a secret marriage.

Lou. And I was weak enough to be persuaded.   Oh, Mr. Single !
you will scorn me —

U. R. *Uncle,* I tell you, child, — *uncle.*   Scorn you ?   Make
your mind easy, my dear.   I 've seen too much of human nature to
scorn any one very easily.   Go on, Ned.

Ed. We had been married about two months, when father suddenly summoned me home.   At the same time, Louisa's mother, a
widow, died.   What could I do ?   I knew no family in which to
place her ; and the thought of separation, at a time when her sor-
rows made her all the more dependent on me, drove me half wild.
I smuggled her into this house, as housekeeper, therefore ; partly to
be constantly near her, and partly, I confess, in hopes that her ami-
ability of character —

Lou. Edward ! —

Ed. Might attract father.

U. R. Ha, ha, ha ! it has, — it has.   Ha, ha, ha !   (*Claps his
hand to his mouth.*)

Ed. What do you mean ?   Explain.

U. R. That is — yes — he 's spoken very favorably of you, my
dear, — very favorably indeed.

Lou. Really ? — really ?   Oh, I 'm *so* glad !

U. R. Trust her to me, Ned ; trust her to me.

Ed. Thank you, uncle.   One word more.   I 'm not to be allowed
to come home oftener than once a fortnight ; and yet I can't bear to
be separated so long from Louisa.

U. R. (*innocently*).   Well, my son —

Ed. That little cottage in the garden, where your room is, Uncle
Robert, is a capital place for a *tête à tête.*

U. R. Why, you young villain !

Ed. My wife will let me know by letter the evenings she is disen-
gaged.   Cottonville is only twenty miles from here, you know.   My
horse can easily do it in a couple of hours.   She comes to your room
through the garden, you see, and I get through the little door in the
wall.   I 've had a key made.   In that way I can talk with my little
wife, without anybody's knowing it.

U. R. (*aside*).   How cleverly the scamp has laid his plans !

Ed. Then you agree, uncle ?

U. R. Child, child, what are you thinking of ?   My duty to your
father ; my conscience.   Such actions as these !   No, no ; it 's out of
the question, — out of the question.

Lou. Dearest uncle —

U. R. Little tease !

Ed. You 'll keep our secret, of course.

U. R. Hem! — well, well, I can't say.

Lou. You 're too kind-hearted to betray us, I 'm sure, uncle.

U. R. You little monkey! Well, I suppose I must submit.

Lou. and Ed. Hurrah! hurrah!

Ed. (x *to* LOUISA). Louisa, dearest, everything will go well now, I 'm sure. I 'm happier than I 've been for a week past. (*Kisses her.*) Keep up your spirits, dear one. I shall see you soon.

U. R. (*aside, wiping his mouth*). *I* might have done that once. Old ass! why did n't you have a little more pluck? (*Slaps his forehead.*)

Ed. Well, my mind 's at ease, now. Good-bye, Uncle Robert ; — see you again soon. (*Going.*) Stay ; — Louisa, dear, your Uncle Bob ; — acknowledged niece, now. Give him a kiss, to prove your gratitude.

U. R. Ah!

Lou. Will you let me, Uncle Robert?

U. R. Oh!

Lou. (*kissing him*). This, with all my heart!

Ed. (*drawing her away*). Now come. Good-bye, uncle, — good-bye.   [*Exeunt* C. D.

U. R. (*shutting his eyes*). By George! lips like velvet! Zounds, how sweet! As clever a lad as ever I saw ; and she 's a charming girl. But his father. Bless my soul! — and William, too. Ha, ha, ha! — and Brownjohn — and Patty — and the flowers — and the Calcutta goods — and the school business — and the jealousy — The deuce! I 'm so cram full of secrets I shall certainly blurt out something. What a complication! I shall go crazy. Thank Heaven, there 's no one else in the house to tell me a secret.

Servant (*opening door*, R. H.) Mr. Single —

U. R. (*starting, and seizing him by the collar*). Rascal! have you a secret, too? — Do *you* want to make me your confidant? — Are *you* in love, too?

Ser. Yes, sir.

U. R. With whom, villain? Speak, villain! — with whom?

Ser. With the cook, sir.

U. R. (*letting him go*). Oh! ah! Ha, ha, ha! lucky fellow.

Ser. Dinner 's ready, sir.   [*Exit* D. R.

U. R. I began to think he 'd fallen in love with Miss Carlyle, too. Ha, ha, ha! (*Sits.*)

END OF ACT I.

ACT II.

SCENE I. — *A garden.* — *House at left.* — *Wall at back of garden.* — *Street beyond.* — *Practical gate in wall.* — *At* R., *front, a rustic arbor, containing table and seat.* — *A statue and shrubbery.*

Enter GRAMPUS *and* UNCLE ROBERT, R. 3 E.

U. R. (L. C.) Grampus, it needs the stomach of a steam-engine, to walk like this, after one's dinner. Don't you know that, at *your* age? You seem in low spirits. Did n't your dinner please you?

Gr. (*growling*). Not a bit.

U. R. Dear me! I'll speak to the cook instantly. (*Going.*)

Gr. Pooh; nonsense; she's not in fault. Have you kept your eye on that infernal puppy?

U. R. What puppy? William's?

Gr. Pshaw! no; I mean that brute Brownjohn.

U. R. Oh! ah! — hem!

Gr. He ogles Louisa the whole time; and he has an infernal knack at complimenting.

U. R. Ha, ha! he knows what he's about. (*Aside, putting hand to mouth*) 'Gad, just saved the secret that time.

Gr. I tell you, Single, he's in love with the girl; and I'd like to kick him out of my house. Single, you'll tell me I'm an old fool, perhaps —

U. R. I? Heaven forbid.

Gr. (*in his ear*). I'm really jealous of that beast of a Brownjohn.

U. R. Jealous! Ha, ha, ha! My dear sir, you may make your mind *perfectly* easy on that score. No danger, I assure you. (*Putting hand to mouth*) Ass that I am!

Gr. How so? What do you mean?

U. R. I mean — I mean — yes — Louisa does n't seem to care for him in the least, as far as I can see.

Gr. I hope you're right, with all my heart. By the way, it's struck me she's been low-spirited, — absent-minded, as it were, — these last three days.

U. R. Ha, ha! of course she has. (*Puts hand to mouth*) Fool! — ass!

Gr. What? Why of *course*?

U. R. I mean — that is — you see — I mean, so many things have to be sent to Ned, that her hands have been full of work the whole time.

Gr. Ay, ay; that indeed. Very likely. Hark'e, Single, I've been thinking over what I said the other day, and I've made up my mind. Sound Louisa's feelings, and if you find her well-inclined to me, why — then —

U. R. You'll marry her?

Gr. Hush; not so loud. If you find she does n't quite hate me, give her this note. (*Gives note.*) I'll have a quiet *tête à tête* with her myself, after she's read it. Write the address on it, if you think best. Be cautious, however, and don't betray my secret.

U. R. Ay, ay, cousin; have no fear. I'll be a perfect fox.

Gr. My fate's in your hands. The ladies will soon be out here. Perhaps you'll find an opportunity then.

U. R. Good. I'll sound her.

Gr. Very well; then, I'll leave you. (*Going. — Comes back.*) By the way, Single, that flower-stealing has n't stopped yet. Last night some of the finest roses in the garden were taken.

U. R. Ha! The graceless little scamp!

Gr. What?

U. R. Oh, noth — nothing.

Gr. I understood you to say —

U. R. Oh no, I did n't — nothing of the kind.

Gr. You said scamp, I thought.

U. R. Oh no. You misunderstood me.

Gr. Single, I'm convinced you know who the thief is. You've betrayed yourself.

U. R. Pooh, pooh, Grampus! — pooh, pooh!

Gr. You do know, I'm certain.

U. R. Why, Grampus — since you — to say the truth — (*Pauses.*)

Gr. What must I infer? And I don't understand William's absence from dinner, for the last three days. He tells me he has your permission. Is that so?

U. R. Hem! — hem! — yes — you see, my dear Grampus —

Enter WILLIAM, *from house, running across garden.*

Gr. William! William, I say! Come here, sir.

Wil. (*down* c.) Did you call me, father?

Gr. Yes sir, distinctly. Explain your absence from dinner, lately, at once. Come.

Wil. Why, sir — the fact is — Uncle Robert —

Gr. Tell the truth, sir. No secrets from me. No lies to your father, sir.

Wil. Of course not, sir. Why, sir — Oh, father —

Gr. There's something behind, here. (x *to* c.) Single, what has William been doing? What's wrong?

U. R. Well, well, Grampus, I've made little Will, here, go without his dinner for three days, as a punishment. There.

Gr. A punishment? His master has been complaining of him again, has he? I'll keep my word, then, sir. You shall go to a boarding-school.

Wil. Oh, father! — Uncle Robert! (*Whispers.*)

U. R. No, no, no, his master has n't said word.

Gr. What is it, then? I insist on knowing. What did you punish him for?

U· R. Because he stole the flowers.

Gr. William?

Wil. Oh, Uncle Robert!

U. R. I found him out, Grampus, and punished him myself, to save you the trouble. That's the whole story.

Gr. So, William, you are the thief.

U. R. Pooh, Grampus, say no more about it. He's been punished enough; and the thing's gone by, now. (*A pause.*)

2*

Gr. Let it pass, then, this time. Never let it happen again, sir. (*Draws* UNCLE ROBERT *aside.*) Play your cards well, now, Single.
[*Exit* R. 3 E.

U. R. (*wiping forehead*). Phew! that job made me sweat!

Wil. But, Uncle Robert, you promised not to tell; and you've just let out the whole to father. It's real mean.

U. R. My lad, I couldn't help it. Secrets are crawling all over me, like catterpillars over an apple-tree. One will drop off now and then. Besides, you scamp, you stole more flowers only last night. (*Seizes him.*)

Wil. No, I didn't, uncle, really and truly.

U. R. Hush; don't lie. Lying boys never prosper. When your father told me that, the whole thing popped out. You've only yourself to thank for it.

Wil. Well, after all, I'm glad it's no worse. Perhaps it's better as it is, after all.

U. R. Yes, rascal, I've lied you out of your scrape this time. I won't do so again.

Wil. (*coaxingly*). Uncle Robert, please tell me your secrets.

U. R. Mind your business, you inquisitive scamp. (*Aside*) It will never do for me to be so absent-minded. Bless me! several of my secrets have almost slipped out already.   [*Exit into house*, L.

Wil. So, that's found out. And shall Louisa have no more flowers? Pooh! who's afraid? The garden is locked at eight, but I can climb over the wall, for I did it last night. Ha, ha! the affair is growing exciting. I wish I knew some trick to play off on that scoundrel Brownjohn. He can't keep his eyes off Louisa. I'd like to throw sand in 'em, hang him! He must annoy her excessively. I'll go and get the boat ready. Perhaps she would like a row on the pond.
[*Exit* L. 2 E.

Enter BROWNJOHN, *from gate*, C.

Brownjohn (*reading from a note-book*).

> May I dare to hope, sweet creature,
> That what I see in every feature
> Is true, and I am loved?
> Or have I erred in so believing,
> And is thy manner but deceiving?
> By scorn art only moved?
>
> No, in those eyes where teardrops swell,
> Truth, only truth can dare to dwell;
> I feel that thou art mine.
> High, higher yet my pulses flout;
> Away with every anxious doubt!
> I feel a bliss divine!

There, for a chap who never wrote a line of poetry in his life, that's not so bad. They've made my head ache like the devil, but they'll please Patty. Where can she be? She promised to meet me here. (*Sits in arbor.*) My position here is intolerable. Compelled to make love to the housekeeper, to hoodwink the father; and yet Patty is as jealous as a cat, and drives me crazy with her suspicions. It's really cruel to Miss Carlyle, now, — really it is. She might very easily fall in love with me, and, when she finds out the real state of things, die of a broken heart. I should never forgive myself, never.

Enter LOUISA, *with embroidery in hand.*

Lou. (*seeing* BROWNJOHN). What, you here, Mr. Brownjohn?
Br. Ah, good day, Miss Carlyle. Always at work, I see.
Lou. I suppose you came to this shady arbor for a nap?
Br. (*coming forward*). A nap? How can anyone think of napping
in a house where your delightful presence —
Lou. Fye, sir; reserve your compliments for a certain young lady
who cares more for them than I do.

Enter PATTY, *from house.* — *She draws back.*

Br. Whom do you mean?
Lou. Do you think, seriously, you can deceive me? As if I didn't
see the real meaning of all your fine speeches. Ha, ha! a little more
sincerity will do you no harm, Mr. Brownjohn.
Br. Miss Carlyle, I assure you —
Lou. No, no, assure me nothing. Perjury is very wicked.
Br. Please explain —
Lou. No; of what use? You understand me very well. Besides,
I've no time to spare. I must leave you now.
Br. Alas! why so soon?
Lou. I find I've forgotten my pattern.   [*Exit into house.*
Br. Can't I get it? (*Sees* PATTY, *who advances.*) Ah! dearest
Patty!
Pat. Delightful, sir. You play your part so *very* well, one can
almost believe you in earnest.
Br. Patty!
Pat. (L.) I left you scarcely five minutes ago, and here you are
making love to Miss Carlyle already.
Br. The merest accident.
Pat. Oh, of course. Accidents happen most conveniently, some-
sometimes.
Br. But Miss Carlyle came to *me.*
Pat. So much the worse, sir.
Br. Patty, how can you imagine —
Pat. I must believe what I see with my own eyes, sir.
Br. (*coldly*). They deceive you greatly, Miss Grampus.
Pat. Deceive me? Did you speak a single word to me all dinner-
time?
Br. No.
Pat. Didn't you talk with Miss Carlyle the whole time?
Br. Yes.
Pat. Didn't you constantly exchange glances with her?
Br. No.
Pat. What! you didn't look at her, I suppose.
Br. I did, but that's not exchanging glances with her.
Pat. Oh, how clever we are, all of a sudden. Did you look at *me*
once?
Br. Yes, indeed, very often.
Pat. You didn't.
Br. Indeed I did; but you refused me a single look.
Pat. Because you're a traitor, — a base deceiver. You join Miss
Carlyle as soon as ever my back's turned.

Br. Patty, 1 cannot endure longer being the object of your ground-less suspicions. I will return when you are more calm, — more just.

Pat. Stay, I command. So you refuse any explanation ?

Br. Yes.

Pat. You refuse to justify your behavior ?

Br. I leave my justification, Patty, to your own good sense — and to your heart.

Pat. (relenting). Mr. Brownjohn —

Br. Your own sense must show you the painful nature of my posi-tion here. I am compelled to feign for another the love I bear for you. I am unskilled in deception, and consequently excite nothing but suspicion on every side.

Pat. (more softly). Julius —

Br. And if you really love me, your own heart will furnish my best apology.

Pat. Julius —

Br. It still beats fondly for me, I'm sure, Patty, in spite of your occasional fits of jealousy and ill-humor.

Pat. Julius, I forgive you.

Br. Ah, darling, thank you. How delightful, to see you reason-able and charming once more !

Pat. Very complimentary. You know, Julius, my jealousy only proves my love.

Br. 'T is a strange love, dearest, which is always paining its object. But I can endure this deception no longer. Can I never get a quiet *tête à tête* with you ?

Pat. Fye, Julius ! how can you ?

Br. Dearest, where is the harm ? Lovers have had *tête à têtes* ever since the world was made.

Pat. Oh dear ! ought I —

Br. Consider now, Patty ; how can we manage it ?

Pat. No, Julius, I cannot — Perhaps in uncle's cottage, yonder. Father always goes out in the evening, and Uncle Robert is sure to be at his chess-club. Oh, I'm certain I shall die — Nobody will inter-rupt us ; for the garden is locked at eight. The gardner will let me in. Oh, Julius ! I can never, never do such a thing, — never.

Br. Capital ! And I ? —

Pat. There's a little door in the wall. I can open it from the in-side. Oh, indeed, indeed, you must n't come, Julius.

Br. (kissing her hand). Charming ! This evening, at eight, then, we will decide how to overcome your father's prejudices.

Pat. My father ! Oh, heavens ! a rock is more easily softened than he is. Hush ! I see him coming. (*Points* R.) Go to him, Julius. He must n't see us together, on any account. I'll meet you again, by the pond, perhaps. Go, go.

Br. Au revoir.   [*Exit* R. 3 E.

Pat. He's a duck of a fellow, after all. I am frightfully cruel to him. (*Looks off.*) He meets father — they are talking together — they have turned. I'll see where they go.   [*Exit* R. 3 E.

Enter WILLIAM, L. 2 E.

Wil. I could n't get the boat ; so Louisa must lose her sail. I wish Patty did n't always insist on going with us. Oh, it must be heavenly to float with Louisa adown the rippling stream.   (*Sees note-book on table.*)   Ah! what's this?   Cards — letters — "*J. Brownjohn, Esq.*" Oh, it's that wretch's.   I mustn't meddle.   Stop; what's this? Poetry.   (*Reads it.*)   Oh! good, — first rate!   Ha! can he have meant it for Louisa?   It must be.   Oh, the villain!   (*About to tear it.*)   Stop; a good idea; — the best revenge I could have.   I'll give it to Louisa myself.   She'll think I wrote it, and admire me immensely; and he'll be cheated of it.   Capital! — two birds with one stone.   (*Tears out verses, and throws note-book under table.*)   Hurrah! what luck!   [*Exit, running.*

Enter PATTY, R. 3 E.

Pat. They've turned again, and are coming this way.   They shall find me in the arbor.   (*An embroidery-frame lies on table.*)

Enter LOUISA, *from house, with pattern in hand. — She thrusts a letter in her bosom.*

Pat. (*in arbor*). Who can Miss Carlyle be working this embroidery for? She has no lover that I know of. Ha! dreadful suspicion! Can it be for Julius?
Lou. (*not seeing* PATTY). Where can Mr. Single be? He promised to take charge of my letter; and there's no time to be lost.
Pat. Hush! There she is. As soon as I see her, all my suspicions return at once.

Re-enter WILLIAM, *running, at side. — He signals to* LOUISA, *throws paper at her feet, puts finger to lip, and exits.*   ·

Pat. What can this mean?
Lou. (*picking up paper*). Verses?
Pat. A letter! I must see this. (*Coming out of arbor*) So absorbed, Miss Carlyle?
Lou. (*starting*). Oh, how you frightened me! I thought no one was here.
Pat. (R.) No one likes to be disturbed, when they *prefer* to be *alone*, of course.
Lou. (L., *laughing*). Have you ever observed, Miss Martha, that I have a preference for solitude?
Pat. Not at *all* times, Miss Carlyle; but you will admit there *are* moments when company is disagreeable.
Lou. Oh, certainly.
Pat. For instance, when one has a private note to read.
Lou. Ah, you saw it, then? One of your brother William's writing-exercises. At least, I suppose so; for if the verses are his own he has no great taste for poetry.
Pat. Verses?
Lou. See for yourself?
Pat. (*taking paper, and recognizing the hand*). Ha! This is abominable!
Lou. (*shocked*). What's the matter?
Pat. Hypocrite! You are detected! You may feign innocence, but I see through your infamous schemes!
Lou. Miss Grampus, I do not understand you.

Pat. What! persist in your hypocrisy! Shameless creature! Is n't this his handwriting?

Lou. Your brother's?

Pat. My brothers! This is *too* much!

Lou. You speak in riddles.

Pat. (*walking about*). Oh, wretch! away with your airs of innocence! They deceive me no longer. But I'll be revenged! — yes, my vengeance shall equal the *contempt* I feel for you both!

Lou. (R.) Can you believe that your brother — a mere boy —

Pat. (L.) Yes, a mere boy; and so all the easier to be hoodwinked.

Lou. Miss Grampus, this accusation —

Pat. How should a mere boy like him know the disgrace of being made a go-between?

Lou. A go-between? I understand you less than ever.

Pat. Ah! here comes father and Mr. Brownjohn. Come here, gentlemen, — come here. I have some wonderful poetry to read to you.

Enter GRAMPUS *and* BROWNJOHN, R. 3 E.

Gr. Poetry, Martha? For Heaven's sake, spare us the trash.

Pat. No, no, father; listen. (*Reads angrily*)

> " *May I dare to hope, sweet creature,*
> *That what I see in every feature*
> *Is true, and I am loved?* "

Br. Ha! what's this? (*Feels in pockets.*)

Pat. Oh, yes, sir, you *may* dare to hope. (*Reads*)

> " *Or have I erred in so believing,*
> *And is thy manner so deceiving;*
> *By scorn art only moved?* "

Br. Where did you get —

Pat. Oh, no, sir, you've *not* erred in so believing. Her manner is *not* deceiving; oh, no!

Lou. (*aside*). I comprehend, now.

Gr. Oh, hush that nonsense.

Pat. No, no, father; hear the rest of it. (*Reads*)

> " *No, in those eyes where tear-drops swell,*
> *Truth, only truth can dare to dwell.*
> *I feel that thou art mine.* "

No doubt you do, sir. (*Reads*)

> " *High, higher yet my pulses flout;*
> *Away with every anxious doubt;*
> *I feel a bliss divine!* "

How beautiful! — " I feel a bliss divine!"

Gr. Martha, these verses are execrable.

Pat. Hush, father; the author is close by.

Gr. What! Mr. Brownjohn, are you the poet?

Br. Your daughter, sir, has thrown me into such embarrassment, that —

Gr. A merchant writing poetical compositions like this? Bad sign, — bad sign.

Pat. Oh, father, it's not at all surprising. So lovely a subject might inspire the stupidest man in the world.

Gr. What? who is the subject?

Pat. Miss Carlyle, sir. She is the object of this sentimental effusion.

Gr. Miss Carlyle! Zounds, sir —

Br. I beg you, sir, let me say two words —

Pat. Why any words? Your deeds speak too plainly. Miss Carlyle received these verses from —

Br. Not from me.

Pat. Not from you? No, but from your go-between, however.

Gr. What? This is a serious charge, Mr. Brownjohn.

Pat. Yes, father, William has been mean enough to act as go-between for Mr. Brownjohn.

Gr. Zounds, Mr. Brownjohn! such conduct as this —

Br. Give me a moment to explain, sir.

Gr. Speak, sir; speak, at once.

Br. (x *to* LOUISA). Miss Carlyle, it gives me much pain to see you suspected in this unpleasant affair; but it is in your power to explain the mystery in one word.

Lou. Sir, to these accusations against my character, my proper defence is to preserve silence. Any other course would be inconsistent with my own self-respect.

Gr. Martha, have you dared to accuse Miss Carlyle?

Pat. Father, on my honor I saw William give these verses to Miss Carlyle. I think, for the reputation of our family —

Br. Miss Grampus, the imputation that I have assailed the reputation of your family is one which I cannot submit to in silence. I declare, on my honor, that these verses were not sent by me to Miss Carlyle, and were never intended for her. They were in my note-book, which I must have left on the table, yonder, and have been taken from it by some unauthorized hand.

Pat. (x, *and hunting about table*). I see no note-book.

Br. This, however, is the explanation of the whole affair, I'm sure.

Gr. But, Mr. Brownjohn, if these verses were not intended for Miss Carlyle, for whom were they intended?

Br. Mr. Grampus — that — that is a secret.

Lou. (*aside to* PATTY). Doubtless for *you.*

Pat. Eh! What?

Gr. Hem! — excuse me, Mr. Brownjohn, if your embarrassment compels me to form an unfavorable view of your conduct.

Pat. (*beginning to understand*). Dear father, perhaps —

Gr. Silence, Martha; this affair is far too delicate to be discussed any longer here.

Br. You are right, Mr. Grampus. I will retire till this unhappy misunderstanding shall have been cleared up. Good afternoon, sir.

[*Exit through gate,* C.

Gr. (*sternly*). Martha, you have probably been hasty; but you have developed a matter which I must examine into more closely. Go tell William to come here at once.

Lou. Let *me* go, Mr. Grampus.

Gr. (*tenderly*). Let Martha go, if you please. (*Sternly*) Go, Martha. (*Tenderly*) I have a few words to say to you, Miss Carlyle.

[*Exit* PATTY, *into house.*

Now, my dear, be frank with me. What do you know of all this ?

Lou. (R.) It's a riddle to me, I assure you, sir.

Gr. Then Mr. Brownjohn did n't send these verses to *you* ?

Lou. No, sir.

Gr. (*tenderly*). And you — you feel — pooh ! you feel no regard for him, eh ?

Lou. Mr. Grampus !

Gr. Nay, nay, dear ; I'm very glad to hear it. Yet it has seemed to me as if — mere nonsense, of course — as if he'd been paying you very great attention, lately.

Lou. I never supposed them to be anything more than the usual gallantry of young men.

Gr. (*very tenderly*). Did you not ? I'm glad to hear it, — delighted to hear it. Let's change the subject. You've noticed, of course, that I am still sound and vigorous, — never ill ; in fact, still in the prime of life ?

Lou. Oh, yes indeed, sir. Heaven keep you so, many, many years !

Gr. (*very tenderly*). Do you wish so ?

Lou. Your whole household wishes so, sir ; and none of them more fervently than I do.

Gr. Ah ! you are a dear, good girl, — an excellent, charming girl ; and if — if — if your affections — if you're not too old for me — I mean — hem ! you do not understand me, I see.

Lou. Why, really, Mr. Grampus —

Enter UNCLE ROBERT.

Gr. Ah ! well, well ; here comes Uncle Robert. He will explain, perhaps. (*Draws him aside.*) Single, make the proposal now. I've been sounding her, and she's just in the humor. Give her my letter. When I come back, give me her answer. (*To* LOUISA) Uncle has a few words to say to you, my dear. Pray give them a favorable answer. *Au revoir.*   [*Exit through gate.*

Lou. (L.) What can he mean. He terrifies me.

U. R. Nothing very terrible, little wifey. It need n't turn your hair gray.

Lou. What have you to say to me, uncle ?

U. R. Shall I give her his letter, or not ? No ; it will only distress her. She'd better never hear of the old fool's folly.

Lou. What can have happened ? Why do you talk to yourself ? Oh, uncle ! relieve my anxiety at once.

U. R. Well, well, my darling, Mr. Grampus is a little bit jealous, that's all.

Lou. Jealous ?

U. R. Don't be alarmed. He's afraid Mr. Brownjohn has fallen in love with you ; nothing more.

Lou. Mr. Brownjohn ? He has no need to be jealous of Mr. Brownjohn.

U. R. I know it, dear, — I know it. Ha, ha, ha ! of course he has n't.

Lou. What do you know ?

U. R. (putting hand to mouth). Blabbing again. That is, my darling, I mean — I think —

Lou. (laughing). No, no, uncle; you've betrayed yourself. You know, I'm certain —

U. R. What, for goodness' sake?

Lou. That Mr. Brownjohn, so far from caring for me, is dead in love with Patty.

U. R. (stopping her mouth). Hush! hush! Who told you that? I never did, did I?

Lou. Why, do you think I'm stone blind?

U. R. What the deuce! I've seen nothing.

Lou. If Patty would only confide a little more in me —

U. R. She'd do so at once, my dear, if she knew you were her sister.

Lou. No, no. It's out of the question, uncle. I cannot tell her.

U. R. Then we must wait till time sees fit to clear matters up, I suppose.

Lou. Yes. At least, I can do nothing without Edward's permission. And, uncle, dear, here's a letter I've written to him. The mail goes at three. Edward will get it at six, and at eight he will be here. I haven't addressed it, for fear my writing might be recognized. Will you do it for me, uncle.

U. R. Certainly. Give it me. (*Takes her by the chin.*) Hold up your head, darling. Don't be frightened. All will end well, depend upon it.

Enter PATTY, *from house.*

Pat. (down C.) Looking to see if Miss Carlyle has the tooth-ache, I suppose, uncle? Fye!

Lou. My dear Martha, a little confidence in my integrity and my regard for you, would put an end to all this misconstruction immediately.　　　　　　　　　　　　　　　[*Exit* L. 3 E.

Pat. Nonsense. Mere pride and vanity.

U. R. Patty, what conduct towards that poor girl!

Pat. Poor girl, indeed! Are *you* bewitched by her arts, too?

U. R. Patty, if you knew — (*Puts hand to mouth.*)

Pat. Knew what?

U. R. Nothing, nothing, my dear. Hem!

*Pat. (*L.) You're very mysterious, Uncle Robert; but you can't persuade me out of what I see with my own eyes.

*U. R. (*R.) Tut! What new ground of quarrel have you had with Brownjohn, Patty?

Pat. Uncle, the best in the world. He's been writing verses to Miss Carlyle. That's sufficient, I think.

U. R. Impossible! It *can't* be, my dear.

Pat. Why not?

U. R. Why, to my knowledge, she cares no more for him than he does for her.

Pat. (delightedly). Oh, uncle! go on, go on.

U. R. Go on? But I've got through.

Pat. No, no. If she doesn't care for Julius, she must be thinking of somebody else; and I wan't to know who it is. You know something, uncle. You've let it out.

3

U. R. (*aside*). How sharp-sighted these girls are! Each sees clean through the other's secret. Amazing! No, no, I don't know anything.

Pat. The other! What other? Can Miss Carlyle have suspected —

U. R. She saw, a long while since, how you and Brownjohn stood towards one another.

Pat. And never told me?

U. R. How could she? How have you behaved towards her? — You've been scornful, suspicious, overbearing. Patty, Patty, is that the way to behave towards a married lady? (*Puts hand to mouth.*)

Pat. Married! Married, did you say?

U. R. Hush! no, I said no such thing.

Pat. Uncle Robert, you shan't escape so. You said *married*. Now, confess the whole story.

U. R. Then don't make such a noise. Hush!

Pat. I insist.

U. R. Well, well, don't speak so loud. Louisa is — has been, I should say — married. She's a widow — probably —

Pat. A widow?

U. R. Yes. It's a sad story. Her husband went to California, two years ago, and she's never heard from him since. Poverty compelled her to go into service.

Pat. Poor creature! And I've done her so much injustice! Dear, dear! — and Julius — oh, I'm *so* glad! And here's his note-book, on the ground, here, just where he said he left it. (*Picks it up.*) William must have found it, the tiresome boy, and brought about all this mischief. Oh, I'm *so* happy!

U. R. Queer thing, woman! Foul weather and fair, rain and sunshine, all in a minute!

Pat. Now, uncle, you must do me a great favor.

U. R. What now?   •

Pat. I promised Julius a *tête à tête*, this evening, at eight o'clock —

U. R. Oho!

Pat. Don't find fault. Lovers have had *tête à têtes*, ever since the world was made, of course.

U. R. Indeed! Oh, there, I haven't a word to say. Where is it to be?

Pat. Never mind where, uncle. Now, Julius has gone away in a rage, and will not come; so I want you to carry a note to the post office for me. You will, uncle; now, won't you?

U. R. 'Pon my word! What next? Am I to be made a go-between, in my old age, for mercy's sake?

Pat. A go-between? How vulgar! You should call it a *postillon d'amour*.

U. R. *Postillon d'amour*. Well, well; the deuce knows, women can always find a pretty name for a naughty thing.

Pat. Call it whatever you like, uncle, dear. I'll run and write my note, at once. You must direct it for me, of course. [*Exit into house.*

U. R. I believe I must sew my tongue into a bag. I've always been famous for caution, everybody knows; but I *do* believe I'm losing my wits. I've almost let out several secrets already.

Enter Servant, from house.

Ser. Mr. Single.
U. R. Well, what is it?
Ser. A man from the telegraph office wants to see you or master, right away, sir. [*Exit.*
U. R. Telegraph! By George! I'd forgotten all about it. One thing drives another right out of my head. Ay, ay, I'll come directly, tell him. [*Exit into house.*

Enter BROWNJOHN, *at gate.*

Br. I hope nobody's here. I want my note-book awfully. Cursed ill luck! (*Hunts about.*) Not here! Some one found it, then. This explains Patty's rage. If I could only get a single word with her. It would be too absurd to go into the house, after leaving it so grandly. Yet her father is away, for I saw him go. No, no, it won't do. What devilish bad luck! She'll not expect me at the *tête à tête*, to-night; so she won't come herself. Hark! is n't that her voice? and her old uncle's, too. They must n't see me here. (*Retires into arbor.*)

Enter UNCLE ROBERT, *with telegram.*

U. R. Tompkins' messenger was in a deuce of a hurry. This must be good for Grampus. Where can I find him? At the broker's office, I suppose, his usual place.

Enter PATTY, *from house.*

Pat. Now, uncle, I depend on you. Here's the note. (*Kisses him.*) There. [*Exit.*
U. R. Well, little tease; I'll see. (*Puts letter in pocket, and going towards gate.*)
Br. Sh — sh —
U. R. (L.) Hey? what's that? Who's here?
Br. (*coming out,* R.) I, sir.
U. R. Ah, Brownjohn! very lucky, this. It saves me a walk. I've a letter for you, from Patty. She wants you to come, all the same, this evening. (*Feels for letter.*) Here. (*Gives telegram.*)
Br. Bravo! let's have it. (*Tears it open.*)
U. R. Ha, ha! what mad folks these lovers are!
Br. (*aside*). What's all this? — "*Recognition of the Southern Confederacy! War! Calcutta goods gone up a hundred per cent! Be quick!*" (*Turns over letter.*) No address. This can't be for me. No matter; it's a great piece of luck. (*Pockets letter.*) I must make haste. Uncle, you've made my fortune! Tell Patty to expect me at eight, without fail. (*Runs off, through gate.*)
U. R. Ha, ha, ha! mad as a March hare! However, young folks are not the only fools in the world. Old boy, don't throw stones. — Little Louisa has bewitched you too. Ass that I am! I might have had just such a sweet little wife, once, myself. Nonsense! what am I dreaming about? I must run and give Grampus this steamer news. (*Going.*)

Enter GRAMPUS, *at gate.*

Gr. (R.) Hallo, uncle; I say, any news for me?

U. R. (L.) News! I warrant you. Tremendous! Here. (*Gives* LOUISA's *note.*)

Gr. (*opening it*). "*This evening — in uncle's room — more when we meet. In the greatest haste — Louisa.* Uncle, you're a jewel. If all goes well, I'll give you a set of chess-men of solid gold. There.   [*Exit into house.*

U. R. Ha, ha! this Calcutta business must be very profitable. Gold chess-men! Well, well; such is man. Queer creatures! Rare world! rare world! Stop, I must get this note to Ned. Louisa asked me to direct it. (*Takes out two letters.*) Zounds! here are two. Oh, ay, this is Grampus's to Louisa. Yes, yes ; I thought best not to give it to her. No address on this, neither. Ha, ha, ha! By the way, which is for Ned? (*Holds them up to light.*) This must be the one, it's so much larger. If I'd changed 'em, there'd have been the deuce and all to pay. Ha, ha! I should never hear the last of it.

[*Exit, laughing.*

(*All four letters must be of same size and appearance.*)

END OF ACT II.

ACT III.

SCENE I. — UNCLE ROBERT's *room in cottage. — Door in flat. — Closet on each side, with curtains. — Bay-window in flat, with curtains. — Clothes on pegs against wall. — Table on* R. *and* L., *with long cloth on each. — Chairs, &c.*

Enter BROWNJOHN *and* PATTY.

Pat. Come in. Gracious, how frightened I feel!

Br. Calm yourself, Patty. There can be no danger. Nobody ever comes here.

Pat. Are you certain you saw who it was ?

Br. Yes; William. He's after flowers, I suppose. I saw him jump from the garden-wall.

Pat. Oh, how dreadful if he were to see us here! And he's no business in the garden, at this time of night. Father forbade his going into it. How fortunate uncle's door was ajar !

Br. Ah, Patty! do you see, now, how much injustice you did me ?

Pat. Hush, Julius. I'm willing, this time, to believe in your innocence.

Br. Believe! Are you not absolutely certain of it? Ought you not to be so, at all times ?

Pat. Ah, Julius! who can trust men ?

Br. But surely you should have confidence in *me*, dearest. Tell me you have, Patty; — tell me so.

Pat. Good gracious, Julius, do you want a confession of my injustice from my own lips, when you have it already in my letter ?

Br. What letter ?

Pat. Why, did n't you receive my letter ?

Br. No, your uncle told me verbally you expected me here this evening; but he gave me no letter from *you.*

Pat. Didn't give you my note?

Br. Then there *was* a note for me? There must have been a mistake made.

Pat. A mistake! Good heavens!

Br. Hush! I thought I heard something.

Pat. Footsteps! (*Runs to window.*) Heavens! it's Louisa!

Br. What can she want here?

Pat. She's coming straight to this cottage. Oh, if she should discover us!

Br. What's to be done?

Pat. We must hide somewhere. We can't escape. There's only one door. (*Runs to closet,* L., *and drops curtain.*)

Br. This is infernal! (*runs to same closet.*)

Pat. Not in here! Heavens!

Br. Where *shall* I go?

Pat. Get behind those clothes; — quick!

Br. Nice position, this! (*Hides in closet,* R. F.)

Enter LOUISA, D. F.

Lou. Not come yet. Can uncle have forgotten to send my note? My position here is dreadful. Edward must confess everything, or take me away. If old Mr. Grampus should put his looks into words everything will come out at once. (*Goes to window.*) A beautiful evening. Edward will have a delightful ride. Ha! who is that? Can it be Edward? No; he is taller. It is William! He's stealing more flowers. The crazy boy will embarrass me terribly, yet, I feel sure. I wish he might be caught. What's that? He starts — looks round. Can there be any one coming? He's running right to this cottage. Good heavens! where can I hide? (*Runs to closet,* R., *and drops curtain.*)

Enter WILLIAM, *with flowers,* D. F.

Wil. Ha! not to be caught so easily. (*Goes to window.*) From here I can see who that was, I guess. And have I climbed the wall, at the risk of my life, to be caught like a rat, at last? Your most obedient servant, sir. Not so fast, if you please. I'd like to know who it is, prowling about the garden. Father's cough, I thought; but what can he be doing here, at this time? If father should catch me, oh, what a wigging I should get! Phew! But *she's* fond of flowers, and no danger shall deter — Jupiter! here's some one coming. (*Runs to* PATTY'S *closet, and lifts curtain. — She pushes him away.*) Patty here! What on earth — Hark! here he comes. (*Crawls under table,* R.) Here's fun!

Br. (*looking out*). Awkward position, this! I can't see a thing. (*Draws back.*)

Wil. Didn't somebody speak? (*Draws back.*)

Enter EDWARD, D. F.

Ed. Nobody here! Where can she be? I must get an explanation of father's mysterious letter. I can't comprehend it. (*Reading letter*) " *Dear Louisa, you have greatly pleased me, and your hap-*

3*

*piness is the fondest wish of my heart. I am of riyil principles, as
you know, but despise prejudice ; and this I will prove to your entire
satisfaction. I ask for a quiet tête à tête with you, where, undis-
turbed, we can discuss matters more fully.*" It's certainly father's hand,
and his illegible signature; but the address is to *me*, and in Uncle
Robert's handwriting. I can't make head or tail of it. The letter is
certainly to my wife. Then how comes it into *my* hands? And what
does it mean, if it *is* to my wife? Can Uncle Robert have let out our
secret, and father mean to tell Louisa he consents ? It looks like it.
Or has father fallen in love with her himself? It's not impossible.
And why has n't Louisa written to me ? I couldn't have stayed in
Cottonville another hour. I wish Uncle Bob would come. Patience,
patience. Hark ! somebody's coming. Here he is, at last. No, that's
father's cough. Zounds ! he's coming straight here ! He must n't
see me here, on any account. Where can I hide ? (*Runs to* LOUISA'S
closet, and starts back. — *She pulls him in.*)

Wil. (*who has watched him*). He's hid, too. Ha, ha ! (*Draws
back.*)

Enter GRAMPUS, D. F. — *Stage darker.*

Gr. (*reading*). "*This evening — in uncle's room. More when
we meet. In the greatest haste — Louisa.*" Well, I never dreamed it
could be done so easily. I thought girls usually hung back a little,
at first; but Louisa, here, jumps at the chance. Humph !— all the
better. It tickles my vanity mightily, too; for she would n't have
been so ready if I had n't taken her fancy. Ha, ha, ha ! The little
witch is cunning, too. *She* knows the place for a *tête à tête*, — trust
her. Single little dreams what's going on in his bachelor quarters.
Ha, ha, ha ! What a face he'd make ! 'T would be as good as a
play. Ho, ho, ho !

U. R. (*without*). Well-managed house, this ! Dog running loose
about the garden. Fine doings !

Gr. The deuce ! there's Single ! What brings him home so early ?
Perhaps he 'll not stay long. I 'll hide. (*Gets under table,* L.)

Wil. Ha, ha ! Now it's complete. All bottled up together, now.
(*Draws back.*)

Enter UNCLE ROBERT, *with bottle in hand.*

U. R. Ha, ha ! check-mated the major, in spite of him. Pity I
could n't stay for another game. But it would never do not to have a
glass of wine ready for Ned, after his ride. No, no. Why don't he
come ? It's growing quite dark. Louisa seems in no great hurry,
either. (*Puts bottle on* R. *table, and lights candle.*) Why, how's this ?
All the curtains down ? I shall stifle. Where's my dressing-gown ?
(*Goes to closet.*)

Gr. (*putting out head*). I hope the old dolt does n't intend to stay.
(*Draws back.*)

Pat. (*seen*). Hush, for Heaven's sake, uncle !

U. R. (*dropping curtain*). Patty ! What the deuce ! — what is she
about here ? and why should I hush ? (*Goes to other closet.* — LOUISA
seen making an imploring gesture.) Oho ! Patty, the minx, gets ear of
this interview, and comes to listen ; and Louisa, seeing her coming,
slips in there. I see. What shall I do, now ? Humph ! — I 'll take

a glass of wine, and pretend not to see. (*Sits at* R. *table, and kicks* WILLIAM). Heavens and earth! there's some one under the table! (*Retreats.*) Can a thief have got in here, and these girls hid themselves? (*Backs against* BROWNJOHN.) Zounds! here's another! I'll run for help. No, it can't be thieves. There's nothing to steal here. Ha, ha, ha! cautious, old boy, — cautious. I'll pretend to go away, and leave them to settle it. (*Opens and shuts door loudly, and creeps behind curtains of bay-window.*)

Wil. (*looking out*). I wish I could cut away. (GRAMPUS *looks out. — They see each other. — A pause.*)

Wil. (*humbly*). Good evening, father.

Gr. What brings you here, sir?

Wil. (*whispering*). I — I — it's only for fun, sir.

Gr. (*crawling out*). Come out, sir. (WILLIAM *comes out.*) What am I to think?

Wil. Noth — nothing, sir.

Gr. What business have you in the garden, at this time of night?

Wil. (*whining*). I'm very sorry, sir.

Gr. The truth, now, sir. No lying! Did you come to steal flowers again?

Wil. (*hiding flowers behind him.*) Of course not, sir. I wanted — I wanted —

Gr. No hesitation, you rascal. Out with it. What did you come for?

Wil. I came, sir — it's only fun, father — I came — to watch Patty, sir.

Gr. Patty! Where *is* she? .

Wil. In there, sir.

Gr. I'll soon settle this business. (*Lifts curtain.*)

Pat. (*humbly*). Good — good evening, father.

Gr. These are fine doings! What brings *you* here, Martha?

Pat. I — I — I —

Gr. Why don't you speak, Miss Grampus. This is very suspicious.

Pat. Oh, father! there's no harm in it, really.

Gr. There's no good in it, or you'd be more ready with your answers. So, this is the way it goes on in my house. Confess the truth, now. Come! quick!

Pat. I — I — I wanted to see what Louisa — Edward —

Gr. Louisa! Edward! Where are they?

Pat. In there, sir.

Gr. What does all this mean? Come out, there! (PATTY x *to* WILLIAM. — EDWARD *and* LOUISA *come out.*) Upon my word! What brings you' rom Cottonville, sir? And you, Miss Carlyle, concealed here with my son. What must I think?

Pat. (*aside to* WILLIAM). Sneak! What did you tell of me for?

Wil. Everybody for number one, Patty. I couldn't help it, really.

Gr. All silent? — No answer?

Ed. (*aside to* PATTY). Malicious creature! to betray us.

Pat. Everybody for number one, Edward. I couldn't help it, really.

Gr. I see I ask in vain. Where's your uncle? All this can't have happened without his knowing of it.

Pat. Yes, sir; uncle will explain everything.

Wil. Yes, father, Uncle Bob's the man.

Gr. Where is he, I say?

Wil. In there, sir.

U. R. (coming out). Good evening, children. (*Rubs hands nervously.*)

All. Uncle Robert!

U. R. Yes, children; I'm not deaf.

Gr. Explain, Single, how it happens —

Ed. You know the whole story, Uncle Robert. Explain this mysterious —

Pat. Uncle Robert, do help us out of this dreadful affair!

U. R. 'Pon my word! here's a vast deal to be done, all in a breath.

All. Speak! — speak!

U. R. Well, well; so be it, then. But first, let me ask how you all came in my room? All silent? Then I must go through you in order. William, how came you in my room?

Wil. I'm the youngest one here, Uncle Robert. You ought to begin with the older ones first.

U. R. The older first, then. Well, Grampus, you're the oldest, I think.

Gr. (taking him aside). Hush! I wrote to Louisa a sort of proposal and asked for an interview; and she agreed to meet me here. (*All retire a little but* GRAMPUS *and* UNCLE ROBERT.)

U. R. Here! Impossible!

Gr. See for yourself. (*Hands letter.*)

U. R. Why, how did you get this?

Gr. You gave it to me yourself.

U. R. I! This was for Ned.

Gr. Edward! How comes Miss Carlyle to be writing such letters as this to Edward?

U. R. Oh! perhaps — it's not for Edward —

Gr. Yes, on second thoughts, it *must* be for Edward. His being here to-night shows there's some secret between them. This letter must have got into my hands by some blunder.

U. R. Blunder! But where's the other, then?

Gr. Other! What other?

U. R. (aside). Here's a nice business! Who can have got the telegram?

Gr. I'm wholly at a loss what to think of all this. What other letter *ought* I to have received? Single, I insist on an answer.

U. R. (aside). All's up, now. All I can say is, that since you received this, Ned must have got the other.

Ed. (coming down L.) Exactly; I have. It was this which induced me to come here to-night.

U. R. (taking letter). Thank goodness! all's safe, then. Look, Grampus — Zounds! what's this?

Gr. (softly). That's my note to Louisa.

U. R. (stupified). So it seems.

Gr. And here's the address, in your handwriting, to Edward.

U. R. Yes — of course — exactly.

Ed. The only meaning I could attach to it was this : I supposed Uncle Robert must have told you the whole story, father, and that you wanted an interview with Louisa, to assure her you had no objection to her poverty, and approved heartily of our marriage.

Gr. Marriage! What! you and Louisa married!

U. R. (*aside to* GRAMPUS). For Heaven's sake, Grampus, get out of this scrape the best way you can. They've been married these three months. This letter of yours has, luckily, two meanings. If it's known you designed Louisa for yourself, you'll be a regular laughing-stock.

Gr. This is horrible!

U. R. (*aside to him*). If you thought her fit to be your wife, you can't refuse her for a daughter. You'd better say *yes*, at once; it's your only course.

Gr. (*raging*). You're right. Uncle has told me all, my children; and though I ought to be very angry with you both —

Ed. Dear father, you forgive us.

Gr. (*joining their hands*). Bless you, my darlings, in Heaven's name — The devil!

Ed. and Lou. Oh, thank you, sir! thank you, a thousand times!

Gr. Kiss me, daughter. And if you love this rascal Edward, here, — whom I suppose I must call home from Cottonville, now, — don't forget his old, cross father.

Lou. Oh, no, sir; never, never! (EDWARD *and* LOUISA *retire.*)

U. R. Aha! this is capital! — capital!

Gr. Capital? Humph! Well, this clears up one mystery. Now what brings Patty here?

U. R. Stay, I must have the other letter in my pocket still. Right, here it is. And now my mind is at ease.

Gr. What letter is this?

U. R. The telegram from New York [Boston — Halifax]. I gave you Louisa's letter instead.

Gr. Confusion! It's too late. It's mere waste paper. What's all this? (*Reads*) "*I have done you an injustice. Come to the garden this evening, and I will explain all. Ever yours — Patty.*"

Pat. Oh, Heavens! it's my letter.

U. R. Your letter?

Gr. Martha, what is the meaning of this? To whom is this written?

Pat. To — to — to —

Gr. Answer me directly.

Pat. To — to — to — Mr. Brownjohn.

Gr. So! But more of this by-and-by. The most important first. Single, where is the telegram?

U. R. I don't know, Grampus. I'm turned completely topsy-turvey.

Gr. The telegram! — hunt for the telegram! (x *to* L.)

Br. (*coming out*). Here it is, sir. Permit me. (*Comes down* R. *of* PATTY.)

Wil. Another one! I wonder if there's any more of 'em.

Gr. And what brings *you* here, sir?

Br. The letter in your hand, sir, was meant for me; but by some mistake Mr. Single gave me this. I opened it hastily, and learnt the news. I saw its value; and I trust to escape your censure for having turned it to account. I bought on time so largely, in consequence, as to be now, probably, a rich man; and may ask, without disparity, for the hand of your adorable daughter.

Gr. Single, Single, what sort of a trick have you played me now?

U. R. Give him the girl, Grampus, and keep the money in the family. Patty loves him, and he's proved himself a sharp fellow. Give him the girl.

Pat. Ah, father, do!

Br. Ah, Mr. Grampus, consider our despair!

Lou. Pray make another couple happy, dear father.

Gr. Hark'e, sir; you've played me a rascally trick, but a sharp one; and I'm determined to punish you. I'll be revenged. Take the girl.

Pat. Dear, darling, nice, good father!

Wil. Well, by Jove! here's a pretty go!

U. R. (*wiping his forehead*). Now there's *two* happy pairs. Who could have expected, at noon to-day, that all these things could have come to pass before the day was out. Grampus, I congratulate you.

Gr. Humph, Single! a nice boggle you've made of this business!

Ed. Kept dark about nothing!

Wil. Blabbed every blessed thing, Uncle Robert!

U. R. Well, well, children, don't be too hard on your old uncle. You gave me too many secrets to take care of. I'm only thankful the troubles of an old bachelor have ended as well as they have. (*To audience*) Would any other lady or gentleman like to make me their confidant? Won't any one step forward? Well, I'm sure! Who could have wound up matters more happily?

SITUATIONS.

PAT.   UNCLE ROBERT.   LOU.   ED.

BR.   WIL.   GRAMP.

R. H.   CURTAIN.   L. H.